Sky the
Unwanted
Kitten

Sky the Unwanted Kitten

Holly Webb

Illustrated by Sophy Williams

For Lucy

STRIPES PUBLISHING
An imprint of Magi Publications
1 The Coda Centre, 189 Munster Road,
London SW6 6AW

A paperback original
First published in Great Britain in 2008
This edition published 2011

Text copyright © Holly Webb, 2008
Illustrations copyright © Sophy Williams, 2008

ISBN: 978-1-84715-213-8

A CIP catalogue record for this book is available
from the British Library.

Printed and bound in China

STP/1800/0007/0911

10 9 8 7 6 5 4 3 2 1

Chapter One

As the car started, Lucy pressed her face up against the window, staring sadly back at her home. Except it wasn't her home anymore. In a few hours' time another family would arrive, and another removal truck, just like the one that was lumbering down the road in front of her parents' car. She blinked back tears as they pulled away, staring back at Nutmeg and Ginger, the two friendly cats from the house next door. They'd been frightened away by all the noise of the removal men, but now they were back on their usual spot, the wall between Lucy's backyard and the one next door. They liked to sunbathe on the bricks, and Lucy loved to play with them and cuddle them and pretend they were hers. She longed to have a cat of her own. She had asked her parents so many times, but they always said she would have to wait until she was older.

The ginger cats stared curiously after the car. Lucy rolled down her window and waved to them. Nutmeg mewed, and walked down the wall toward the street. Lucy sniffed miserably.

She couldn't believe she would never see them again. A few seconds later the car turned out of her street and she could no longer see the cats, or even the house.

"How long till we get there?" Kieran, Lucy's older brother, asked, unplugging his new iPod for a moment.

"A couple of hours, probably," their mom said. "We should definitely be settling in by lunchtime!"

"Doesn't it feel great, being on our way to our new home!" their dad added enthusiastically.

Lucy sniffed and said nothing. She clutched Stripy, her old toy cat, even tighter. They'd just left her home behind. What they were going to was only a horrible *house*. It would never, ever be home.

Lucy hardly spoke the whole journey. She just gazed out of the window, and worried to herself. A new house. A new school. No friends! She missed Ellie, her best friend, loads already. Ellie would be in the middle of PE right now. *I wonder if she's missing me too?* Lucy thought.

"We're almost there!" her mom said excitedly, jerking Lucy out of her daydream, where she was back at school playing soccer with Ellie. "Look, Lucy, this is our street! Doesn't it look nice?"

Lucy made a small *mmm* sort of noise. It was nice. Pretty yards and friendly-looking houses. But it wasn't home.

"Oh good, the removal men are here already! Let's start getting unpacked. I bet you two want to see your rooms, don't you?" Dad sounded even more enthusiastic than Mom, if that was possible.

Lucy's new room was huge—much bigger than her old one, as Mom had happily pointed out. "And you can have it any color you like, Lucy," she promised, placing a box of toys on the floor. "Maybe purple, what do you think?"

Lucy sat on the bed that the removal men had dumped in the corner, and gazed around, hugging Stripy. She was trying to be happy, but it was all so different.

The weekend flew past in a messy, grubby whirl of unpacking. Lucy felt left out—Mom and Dad were so happy about the move, and even Kieran was excited about the new house. She seemed to be the only one who missed home.

Now the moment she was really dreading had arrived—her first day at her new school. Surely someone who'd just moved ought to get at least a week off school, not just one Friday, spent driving to the new house. Even Kieran had complained that it wasn't fair they had to start their new schools today. Lucy trailed slowly across the empty schoolyard after her mom, who was heading for the school office.

"Look!" Mom said brightly. "That sign says they have a gardening club. You'd love that, helping to plant seeds, wouldn't you?"

"Maybe," Lucy murmured. She saw a notice up about a soccer team, too, but there was no way she'd be able to join a team now, in the middle of term. *Everyone will already have their friends, and their gangs,* she thought unhappily. *I'm going to be so left out.*

The school secretary buzzed them in and took them over to Lucy's classroom. The school was actually much newer and smarter than the one Lucy had been going to until three days before, but she wished she was back at her scruffy old school. She stayed silent as her mom and the secretary chatted about the new computer suite. Her mouth was drooping sadly as they arrived at class 5W, and the secretary showed them in.

Her new teacher, Mrs. Walker, smiled kindly at her, then announced, "Class, I'd like you to meet Lucy. She's just moved here, and I want you all to make her feel very welcome."

Lucy blushed and didn't know where to look. She hated everyone staring at her. Mrs. Walker then took Lucy to one side, and said the class had really been looking forward to having her and she knew Lucy would be very happy once she'd settled in.

Lucy wasn't sure how she was supposed to do that—she'd never had to settle in anywhere before. She'd been to the same school since nursery, and she had known *everyone*.

"You sit here, Lucy, and Orla and Katie will look after you," Mrs. Walker said. "You'll show Lucy where everything is, won't you, girls?"

Orla and Katie nodded and smiled. "Hi, Lucy!" they chorused.

"Hello," Lucy muttered, and sat

down as quickly as she could.

Orla and Katie tried their best, but Lucy was too shy to give more than yes or no answers to their polite questions. Eventually they gave up, and although they stayed with her all through the lunch hour, they stopped bothering to talk to her. *They don't like me*, Lucy told herself unhappily, as she listened silently to Orla telling Katie all about her ballet exam. *No one's even talking to me.*

Class 5W were actually quite a friendly group, but they couldn't do much faced with a silent Lucy, and she was so unhappy that she couldn't see that she needed to make an effort, too. Lucy was in the locker room putting on her coat to go home, when she heard some of the girls talking about her. She stayed frozen where she was, hidden behind a coat-rack, and listened.

"That new girl is a little strange," someone said, giggling.

"Yeah, she hardly said a word all day." Lucy recognized the voice of Orla, one of her minders. "I hope Mrs. Walker doesn't make us look after her tomorrow as well."

"Perhaps she thinks she's too good for us," another voice suggested. "I'm glad I didn't have to talk to her."

"Yeah, she does seem a little stuck-up," Orla agreed.

Another girl from Lucy's class who was on the same side of the locker room as her gave Lucy a worried look, and coughed loudly. There was a sudden silence, then Orla's head popped around the coats, and her eyes went saucer-wide. She shot back again, and there was a burst of embarrassed giggling.

Lucy stood up and stalked out, blinking back tears. So what if they didn't like her? She certainly didn't like *them*. She heard the girls start whispering very fast, worrying about her telling Mrs. Walker what they'd said. *I hate this school*, she thought, as she brushed her sleeve across her face angrily, trying to pretend to herself and everybody else that she wasn't crying.

"So how was your first day? Did you have a good time?" her mom asked eagerly as she met Lucy at the school gate.

"No. It was horrible, and I want to go home."

"Oh, Lucy, I'm sorry." Her mom looked at her anxiously. "I'm sure it'll get better, honestly. You just need to take a few days to get used to everything." She sighed, and then said in a cheerful voice, "I thought we'd walk back, it's not far. Kieran wanted to go by himself, so you and I can see if we spot any nice parks on the way home."

"Not there, *home*. I want to go back to our old house, and my proper school. I hate it here! No one likes me!" Lucy wailed. "I miss Ellie, and all my friends!"

Mom sighed again. "Lucy, your dad and I have explained this. We had to move. Dad's job is here now, and if we lived in our old house, he'd have to spend hours getting to work. We'd never see him. You wouldn't like that, would you?"

Lucy shook her head, and sniffed, trying not to cry where loads of people from school would see her. "I know," she whispered. "But it's really horrible here."

Her mom put an arm around her shoulder. "I know it's hard, sweetheart. But I promise it *will* get better. We'll just have to do lots of fun things to cheer you up."

Lucy rubbed her sleeve across her eyes. She couldn't believe she had to go back tomorrow.

Chapter Two

Lucy stared out of the classroom window, trying not to catch anyone's eye. She'd been at her new school for nearly a week now, but she still hadn't settled in. She couldn't forget the way Orla had talked about her. The awful thing was, Lucy knew she probably had seemed stuck-up and unfriendly, and all those things Orla had said. But it still seemed unfair. Didn't they know how lonely she was? Couldn't they see how difficult it was being the new girl? *At least it's Friday*, Lucy thought.

"Hey! Pssst…"

Lucy jumped slightly as someone prodded her hand. She looked up, confused. The pretty red-haired girl who sat across the table from her in her math group had poked her with a pencil.

"Mrs. Walker's watching you," the red-haired girl whispered. "If you weren't new, she'd have gotten mad at you by now. You've been looking out of the window for ages and we're supposed to be drawing that hexagon shape. Are you stuck? Do you need a rubber or something?"

Lucy shook her head, and gave her a tiny smile. "I'm OK, thanks," she whispered back, glancing quickly over at Mrs. Walker. It was true—the teacher was looking her way. She bent her head over her book, suddenly feeling a little less miserable. Maybe there were some nice people in her new class after all.

When the bell rang for recess, Lucy watched as the red-haired girl wandered out of the classroom with a group of other girls, all chatting excitedly. Maybe she should say something to her? But that would mean going up to her in front of the whole group. She would have to try to say something interesting, or just hang around on the edge of the circle until someone noticed her. She couldn't face that, what if they all ignored her? Lucy gave a little shudder and stayed put. She'd go to the school library. Like she had every other day this week.

The next morning, Lucy lay in bed, hugging Stripy, and feeling grateful that she didn't have to drag herself out to get ready for school. She'd tried to go back to sleep, but it wasn't working. She sighed, and looked around her room. So far she hadn't even bothered to unpack all her boxes. She was still hoping that somehow things would change and they could go home, but the hope was draining away with every day they stayed.

Kieran wasn't helping, either. He was loving his new school, and last night he'd spent most of dinner time talking enthusiastically about going to play soccer with some really cool new friends he'd made already. Mom was really excited about all the decorating that needed doing, and Dad had started his new job… Only Lucy was desperate to go back to their old home.

"Lucy! Hey!" It was Kieran, banging on her door.

Lucy ignored him, but he didn't go away. "Lucy! Get up, lazy!" He opened her door a crack, and peered in.

Lucy sat up. "Out! You're not allowed in my room!"

"OK, OK! But get up. Mom and Dad have got a surprise for you in the kitchen. You're going to love it!" he called, then thumped off back downstairs again.

A surprise! For a tiny moment Lucy's heart leaped. They were going home after all! She jumped out of bed and raced down after Kieran.

"Are we going home?" she gasped excitedly, catching him just at the bottom of the stairs.

Kieran gave her a strange look. "Of course not, silly, this *is* home now."

Lucy's shoulders slumped again. She trailed into the kitchen after him.

"Lucy!" Her parents were smiling happily at her, which just made Lucy feel more alone than ever.

"We've got a surprise for you, darling. Remember we said you'd have a special treat when we moved here?" Mom pointed to a large box on the kitchen table.

Lucy stared dully at it. When her parents told them about the move, they'd said they would get Kieran an iPod, and that they had a special present in mind for Lucy, too. She'd been so sad missing everyone at home that she'd forgotten all about it.

She stared at the box, feeling just a little excited. What could be inside? Suddenly the box started squeaking.

Lucy moved closer, curious despite herself. She opened the top flaps, which were attached together to make a sort of handle, and peered in.

Inside the box was the most beautiful creature Lucy had ever seen. A kitten with soft creamy fur, huge blue eyes, a chocolate-brown nose and wonderful oversized brown ears.

Lucy gasped. A kitten!

The kitten looked anxiously up as the box opened, and mewed. It was a strange noise, almost like a baby crying, and Lucy immediately wanted to pick up the kitten and cuddle it. The kitten seemed to think this was a good idea, too. It stood up, balancing its paws on the side of the box, and shyly put its head over the side, looking up at Lucy with its amazing sapphire-blue eyes. "Wowl?" it asked pleadingly. "Wowl!"

Lucy lifted out the kitten, and it immediately snuggled into her pajama top and started to purr. "Hello, little one," she said softly.

"Told you she'd love her," Lucy's dad said happily to her mom. "She's called Sky, Lucy. She's a Siamese. We know you've wanted a kitten for so long, and we think you're old enough now to look after a cat properly."

"Yes," said Mom. "We know how upset you've been about us moving to Fairford. But you can't be miserable with a beautiful kitten to play with, can you?"

Lucy stared at them in disbelief. The kitten was sweet, but it was as if her parents thought having a pet would suddenly make everything all right again. Lucy would forget about Ellie and all her friends, her school, her old bedroom, and be happy forever. Her eyes filled with angry, disappointed tears.

She carefully detached the kitten's tiny, needle-sharp claws from her pajamas, and put her back in the box. Then she ran out of the kitchen, her shoulders heaving.

"Lucy!" Mom called after her, her voice shocked.

"Hey, Lucy, what's the matter?" Kieran said. "Mom, Dad, can I pick the kitten up? It's really cute, and it's crying."

Dad's voice was worried as he answered. "Yes, give her a cuddle, Kieran. I need to go and talk to Lucy, and find out what's wrong. I just don't understand, I was sure she'd be so happy."

Chapter Three

Lucy's dad had picked up Sky from the breeder early that morning. Sky had only left home before to go to the vets, and she'd always returned to her familiar room, and the big basket she shared with her mom and her brothers and sisters. Today she'd had to stay in the dark box on her own for ages, and she was so lonely. She wished she could go home, and snuggle up and let her mom lick her fur to make her feel better.

Where was she? It didn't smell like the vet's, and it certainly wasn't home. She couldn't hear any other cats, either. She had started to cry for her home and her mom, and then someone had opened the box.

Sky shrank back into the corner of the box and peered up at the girl, feeling scared. Who was this? It wasn't one of the people she had met before. But then the girl, Lucy, had picked her up, and Sky had relaxed a little. She could see the delight in the girl's eyes, hear it in her quickened breathing, and feel it in the thud of her heart as the girl held her close. She had nestled snugly up against her, purring gratefully. She liked this person. The girl had petted her, and nuzzled her ears, and rubbed her lovingly under her chin. But then suddenly she had taken her firmly around the middle, and put her back into that dark box.

Sky didn't understand. She had *felt* how happy the girl was to hold her. Lucy had been full of love, she knew it. So why had she suddenly changed her mind? The soft, cuddly person had turned stiff and irritable, and Sky didn't know why.

Now she was sitting in a large, comfortable basket in the corner of the kitchen, with a bowl of kitten food and another bowl of water. There was a litter tray close by. She had everything she needed. But no one was with her, and she was so lonely. What had she done wrong? When Lucy had ran out, the boy had cuddled her briefly, then everyone had disappeared, and the kitchen was empty.

Sky was not used to being on her own. Until early this morning, she had lived in a house that was full of cats—her mom, and all her mom's sisters and their kittens, and her own sisters and brothers. There was a whole room full of boxes and big scratching posts and toys. Sky had spent most of her time with her mom, snuggling up in their basket, but she enjoyed being petted and picked up by people as well.

She wouldn't have minded leaving her home so much if Lucy had stayed cuddling her, but now she was alone she felt desperate to go back. She howled her loud, piercing Siamese howl, crying for someone to come and love her.

Upstairs in her room, Lucy could hear Sky. The kitten's sad, lonely wails made her want to cry, too. She knew exactly how Sky felt—taken away from her nice home, and brought somewhere she didn't belong. She wished she could go and comfort her, but she just couldn't do it.

Lucy could hear her parents coming up the stairs, talking in low, worried voices, and she knew she had to explain how she was feeling. The trouble was she wasn't sure she *could*. Maybe it would be easier just to say she'd changed her mind about wanting a cat?

Her parents came in, and sat next to her on her bed. Her mom put an arm around her, but Lucy sat stiff and tense.

"I'm sorry, but I don't want a kitten," she said tiredly when Dad asked what was wrong.

Her parents exchanged confused glances. "But Lucy, you've begged for one for years!" Mom protested. "Every Christmas and birthday, a kitten's been top of your list. Now we've finally moved to a house big enough to have a cat, and on a nice quiet street, and you've changed your mind!"

"Yes, I've changed my mind," Lucy echoed.

"We thought you'd love a kitten," Dad said, shaking his head. "I just don't understand. All that time you used to spend playing with Nutmeg and Ginger next door. Mrs. Jones used to joke that they were more your cats than hers."

Lucy's eyes filled with tears again at the thought of Nutmeg and Ginger. She missed them so much.

There was another mournful cry from downstairs. "That poor kitten," Mom said. "She doesn't know what's going on. We'd better go down so she isn't all on her own. Lucy, I know you're missing our old home, but we thought Sky would cheer you up. She really needs someone to look after her."

Lucy didn't answer, and kept her eyes fixed firmly on the floor. She knew that! She was desperate to go and cuddle Sky, and tell her everything would be all right. But things weren't all right, and it was no use pretending.

Lucy glanced up as her parents closed the door. As soon as she was sure that they were both at least halfway down the stairs, she buried her head in her pillow and cried and cried. A kitten! At last! And she couldn't keep her!

Eventually, Lucy dragged herself up from her bed. She wanted someone to talk to—she wanted Ellie! Lucy took out a pen and her favorite cat writing paper from one of the boxes, and started to write to her about everything.

Hi Ellie!

Mom and Dad have just given me a beautiful Siamese kitten! She's so cute and soft to cuddle, and she's got the biggest blue eyes you've ever seen. I should be really happy, but the thing is I can't keep her! They think giving me a kitten will make me cheer up, and not miss home and you and all my friends. Mom even said so! Well, that's not going to happen.

Lucy started to cry again, and her tears smudged the ink on the page. She scrunched up the unfinished letter and threw it in the wastebasket. It was just so unfair! A beautiful kitten, just like she had always wanted, but her parents had only got Sky to make Lucy forget her real home.

"Well, I won't!" Lucy muttered fiercely, gulping back sobs. "They can't make me! Not even with a kitten…"

By now Lucy had cried so much that she was desperately thirsty, and her head ached. She threw on some clothes, and opened her bedroom door quietly. Kieran had gone out to play soccer, and Mom and Dad were in the backyard, looking at the rickety old shed. She could creep down and grab a glass of juice without having to talk to anyone.

Upstairs in her room it had been terribly difficult to tell herself she didn't want a kitten. Downstairs in the kitchen, with Sky staring at her with huge, confused, sad blue eyes, it was completely impossible. Lucy held out for as long as it took to go to the fridge and pour her juice, and drink a few thirsty gulps. But the sight of Sky lost in her too-big basket was irresistible. Lucy put the glass on the table and knelt down beside Sky.

"You don't know what's going on, do you?" she asked gently. "I'm not trying to be mean, honestly," she sighed.

Sky just wanted someone to play with her. She stood up, stretched, and put a paw on Lucy's knee. She gazed at her, her head on one side questioningly. "Maaa?" she mewed pleadingly. Lucy's mom had left a cat toy in the basket, a little jingly ball with ribbons attached to it, and Sky pawed at it hopefully.

Lucy shook her head, smiling. "OK. When it's just you and me, I'll play. But we have to pretend, all right? When Mom and Dad are around, I won't be able to play at all." She looked at Sky. She knew a kitten wouldn't understand that sort of thing, even if she did look very intelligent.

Sky batted at the ball again. Enough talking. She wanted to play.

Lucy danced the ribbons in front of Sky, bouncing the little ball up and down, and sending Sky in crazy, skittering circles all over the kitchen. It was so funny! Lucy hadn't known Nutmeg and Ginger when they were kittens, and she hadn't realized how much more playful a little kitten would be than her two middle-aged, rather plump cat friends. Sky danced, she jumped, she tumbled over and over, attacking the fierce ribbons. "Oh, Sky!" Lucy giggled.

Then she heard voices coming up the walkway. Mom and Dad! Swiftly she stood up, and dropped the jingly ball back into Sky's basket. Sky watched her, puzzled. Was this a new game? Was she supposed to jump into the basket and pull it out again? She dived in, and popped up with a mouthful of ribbons. But Lucy had turned away. She was standing by the table, drinking her juice. Sky waited. Maybe she was supposed to creep up on Lucy, and give her a surprise? Yes! It was a hunting game! She dropped the ball and leaped sneakily out of her basket. Tummy low to the ground and ears pricked with excitement, Sky crept across the kitchen floor—slowly, slowly, now pounce on Lucy's foot!

Just then, Lucy's parents came back into the kitchen. They saw Sky standing on her hind legs, her paws on Lucy's jeans, gazing pleadingly up at her. Lucy was ignoring the kitten entirely, not even looking at her.

Lucy's mom sighed, and went to pick Sky up and pet her. Sky gave a tiny purr —it was nice to be cuddled—but she was still gazing at Lucy. She was confused. Why didn't Lucy want to play anymore? What had gone wrong? It was as though Lucy was a different person. And not a very friendly one.

Chapter Four

By Monday morning, Sky was even more confused. Lucy gave her lots of cuddles and was wonderful to play with when they were on their own, but as soon as anyone else came into the kitchen, she would pretend that she couldn't even see Sky. It was horrible. Sky couldn't help feeling that she must have done something wrong, and she was desperate to make it better. Lucy's mom was trying to keep her in the kitchen until she settled in, but Sky had other ideas. She wanted to follow Lucy everywhere. She trailed determinedly around the house after her, and tried to climb into Lucy's lap every time she sat down.

Lucy was sat at the table eating breakfast, so she tried it again now. But Lucy gave her one quick, unhappy glance and slid her off. Sky crept back to her basket, her whiskers drooping. Kieran made a huffing noise at Lucy, as though he thought she was being stupid. "Here, Sky," he murmured, holding out his hand. "Kitty, kitty."

Sky sniffed his fingers politely, but it

was Lucy she really wanted. She gave him a little purr as he tickled her ears, though. Then she looked up hopefully at Lucy one last time, but she was staring firmly at her cereal bowl.

Lucy's mom was watching them as she buttered some more toast. "We've got to be really careful not to let Sky out of the house today when our new sofa is delivered. She isn't big enough to go outside yet."

Lucy shrugged and saw her mom give her a worried look—she was obviously thinking that Lucy still hadn't changed her mind about Sky. She stared into her cereal, not feeling hungry. Things were going just as she'd planned, and she'd never felt so miserable.

School seemed even worse on Monday. A few times during lessons Lucy glanced at the red-haired girl, hoping she would look back, but she never did. It would be so good to have *someone* to talk to, and the red-haired girl—Lucy was pretty sure she was called Izzy—had seemed friendly before.

At home time Lucy trailed silently down the street after her mom.

"Did you meet anyone nice today?" her mom asked cheerfully.

"No," Lucy sighed. "There *isn't* anyone nice."

"Oh." Her mom looked upset, and Lucy felt a little guilty.

Lucy glared at the new house as they turned into their street. Then she grinned. Sky was perched on the back of the new sofa in the living room, peering out. Lucy blew her a kiss behind her mom's back as Mom fumbled for her keys, and Sky made a flying leap off the sofa. Eventually, Lucy's mom opened the door, and Sky shot out...

"Oh, catch her, Lucy! We mustn't let her go into the road!"

Lucy tried to grab the kitten, but Sky was too fast for her. Sky danced about all over the yard, enjoying the game of chase. She hadn't had any time with Lucy today, and now Lucy was giving her lots of attention! She hid behind a large plant, her tail swishing excitedly, waiting to jump out.

"Sky! Here puss, puss…" Lucy was creeping closer, hoping to take the kitten by surprise and grab her. She could see Sky's whiskers twitching from behind those big leaves. She jumped behind the plant and her hands closed on nothing as Sky clambered onto the wall.

"I'll go and get some cat treats," Lucy's mom said. "Just try to keep her in the yard, Lucy, please!"

"Oh, Sky," Lucy whispered, as Mom disappeared into the house. "I know I haven't been very nice, but don't run off, please. Come on…"

Sky stretched out to sniff Lucy's fingers as Lucy moved slowly closer. Lucy's eyes were bright and wet, and she looked so sad. Sky rubbed her head against Lucy's hand, hoping to cheer her up, and Lucy smiled a little.

"You're just so beautiful," Lucy murmured, as she scooped the kitten gently off the wall and into her arms. She brushed her cheek against Sky's face, and Sky purred happily.

Gazing down the street, Lucy blinked in surprise. There was Izzy! Just turning the corner, with a bigger girl who had the same red hair. They looked so alike that they had to be sisters. Did Izzy live in this street, too? Lucy watched hopefully as the two girls walked along the other side of the street, and stopped at a house a couple of doors down. Izzy suddenly looked around and caught Lucy's eye, and Lucy blushed, embarrassed to be caught staring.

Izzy gave Lucy a quick smile and a tiny wave, almost as though she was shy, too. Then she followed her sister up the walkway.

Lucy held Sky close, imagining how great it would be to have a friend living just across the street. They could walk to school together. Maybe have sleepovers at each other's houses. She'd always gone by car to her old school, and none of her friends lived anywhere close, not even Ellie. Without thinking, she rubbed Sky gently behind the ears, making her close her eyes and purr with delight.

"So you caught her then?" Lucy's mom was now standing right beside her, holding a bag of cat treats, and smiling.

Lucy looked up, still lost in her thoughts. Then she remembered. Ellie was her friend, not Izzy. She didn't want a kitten to make her forget. She didn't want a kitten at all. She'd told her parents that. She stuffed Sky into Mom's arms, and dashed into the house.

But she could hear Sky mewing, and she longed to rush back and cuddle her again.

Chapter Five

Lucy was staring gloomily at the bean plants in the school garden, and wondering why they bothered growing beans when nobody liked them. Suddenly, somebody tapped her on the shoulder and she jumped.

Izzy grinned at her. "Sorry to scare you. I guess you didn't hear me coming up behind you!"

"Um, no," Lucy murmured.

"I'm Izzy. Do you live in our street, Hazel Street? I saw you yesterday on the way home from school." Izzy stared eagerly at Lucy.

Lucy nodded. "Yes, we've just moved there," she said quietly.

Izzy didn't seem too bothered by Lucy's flat tone of voice. "That's great. There's no one else my age in our street—well, only Sean Peters and he's worse than no one. It'll be really good to have another girl around."

Lucy smiled. It felt so nice to be wanted!

"So is that beautiful kitten yours? Is she a Siamese? Have you had her long? You're so lucky, having a kitten!"

Lucy said nothing. She didn't know

what to say. Sky was her kitten, but she wasn't going to be keeping her, was she?

Lucy stared at the ground. There was an uncomfortable silence. Izzy turned to go.

"Orla said you were stuck-up," she said. "I told her you might just be shy, but maybe she was right." She shrugged, and marched off across the garden.

Lucy stared after her, her thoughts racing. Izzy was really nice, and seemed to want to be friends. But now she thought that Lucy was stuck-up. As Izzy opened the gate to the yard, Lucy dashed after her, trampling most of a row of carrot plants in her rush to catch her up. She caught hold of Izzy's sleeve.

"I'm really sorry, I'm not stuck-up, honestly. I just didn't know what to say." She sighed.

Izzy just looked at her. It wasn't a very encouraging start, but Lucy took a deep breath and began to explain.

"Look, I *really* didn't want to move here. We had to because of my dad's job. I just kept hoping and hoping that my mom and dad were going to change their minds. It's not that I don't think Hazel Street is nice," she added quickly, not wanting to be rude about Izzy's home. "And I guess this is probably a nice school, but I'm really missing my old school, and it's just not the same."

Lucy stopped for breath. Izzy looked curious, so she kept going. "Mom and Dad are trying to persuade me to like it here. They gave me Sky on Saturday, to make me feel better about the move. That's what Mom said." Lucy's eyes filled with tears. "She's supposed to help me forget my old house and my friends and everything."

"Wow," Izzy muttered. "I suppose I'd be miserable if I had to move somewhere totally new."

Lucy nodded.

"But at least you have Sky. She's beautiful!" Izzy smiled.

"She is," Lucy agreed. "You're going to think I'm stupid. But—well, I'm pretending I don't like her. That's why I just didn't know what to say when you asked if she was my kitten."

Izzy looked confused. "But why?"

"If Mom and Dad see I really love Sky, they'll think I've stopped missing home and I don't mind staying here," Lucy explained. It *did* sound stupid. She blushed miserably.

"I *guess* that makes sense," Izzy said

rather doubtfully. "So your mom and dad think you don't want her?"

"Whenever they're around I don't play with Sky, or even look at her," Lucy admitted.

Izzy nodded slowly. "But what's going to happen? If your parents think you don't want her, won't they give her back? You're going to let them?"

"Yes. I mean, I thought I was. I was missing home so much." Lucy sat down on the bench by the gate, and heaved a huge sigh. "Only now I'm not sure I can!"

"Mmmm." Izzy sat down next to her. "I can't imagine giving her back. She's so cute!"

Lucy smiled. "She is, isn't she?" Then she put her chin in her hands and sighed again. "But I can't just change my mind now…"

"You might end up having to stay here, *and* not having a beautiful kitten," Izzy pointed out.

"I know," Lucy said gloomily.

That night, Lucy waited until her parents were both in the living room, and then crept out of bed. She stole quietly down the stairs, not wanting Kieran to hear her either, and along the hallway to the kitchen.

Sky looked up hopefully as she opened the kitchen door. Lucy had petted her quickly a few times that evening when no one was looking.

She did wish that Lucy would be nice like that all the time. Sky waited anxiously. Was Lucy going to ignore her again?

Lucy came and sat down next to her basket, and gently petted the top of Sky's silky head. "Izzy thinks I'm stupid not telling Mom and Dad how much I like you," she told the kitten. "She said she doesn't know how I can pretend. I'm not sure I know either," she added sadly.

Sky climbed out of her basket and clambered up Lucy's leg. She stood on Lucy's lap and butted her chin. That was sure to make her feel better. She licked Lucy, too, just to be certain. There.

Lucy giggled. "Oh, Sky, your tongue's really rough!"

Sky purred as she heard Lucy laughing. It had worked. Lucy was feeling better. She'd seemed so sad before, but now she felt warm and friendly. Sky curled herself into a comfortable ball on Lucy's knee, gave a huge yawn and went to sleep.

Chapter Six

Sky woke up and yawned, stretching her paws lazily. Then she opened her eyes wide, remembering where she was. Lucy's house. The thought of Lucy made her sit up eagerly. Lucy! Where was she? Last night Lucy had cuddled her to sleep on her knee— but now she was back in her basket. Sky hopped out and went to sniff at the kitchen door. She looked up at the handle thoughtfully. Her mom could jump and open door-handles, but Sky wasn't big enough yet. She prowled up and down impatiently. Maybe Lucy would be down soon, and she'd have someone to play with.

When Lucy's mom came downstairs, Sky wove around her feet, nearly tripping her up, but Lucy's mom just laughed. "Are you starving, Sky? Poor kitten! Here you go." She placed a full bowl of kitten food on the floor, and Sky settled down to eat it, keeping one eye on the door.

When Lucy finally came into the kitchen, Sky danced over to her delightedly. *Where were you? I've been waiting for you! Cuddle me!* she mewed.

Lucy gulped. She cast one quick glance at Sky, her tail pointing excitedly straight up, her whiskers twitching with happiness, and then dragged her eyes away. It was so unfair to keep doing this! Sky didn't understand that she could only love her when no one was around. *Quite soon,* Lucy thought sadly, *Sky's going to give up on me.*

Lucy's parents watched as the kitten pawed eagerly at Lucy's leg, and Lucy ignored her again. Lucy's dad gave her mom a serious look and shook his head.

Sky gazed up at Lucy. After last night, she'd been sure that Lucy wouldn't act all strange and cold again. Her tail hung low now as she slunk miserably back to her basket, ignoring the rest of her food.

Lucy didn't touch her breakfast either.

"Wow, you must be starved," Izzy said, watching Lucy munching swiftly through an apple at break.

"Mmmm," Lucy nodded, swallowing. "Didn't eat much for breakfast."

"Well, we have PE straight after, so you'd better have this as well." She reached into her bag and pulled out a cereal bar.

Lucy gave her a grateful look. "Don't you want it?"

"No. Mom keeps giving me them, but they're yuck. You're welcome," Izzy smiled.

Lucy had looked for Izzy as soon as she arrived at school that morning, hoping that she would be there already. She'd been delighted when Izzy had seen her and rushed over. When they entered the classroom, Izzy had asked if she wanted to sit next to her—there was room, and she said Mrs. Walker wouldn't mind. Orla and Katie looked surprised, but they didn't say anything.

"Hello," Lucy muttered shyly, as she went past. It was the first thing she'd said to them since her first day, and they looked a little confused.

It was amazing how different school was now she had someone to talk to. Lucy found she actually enjoyed their PE lesson, which was soccer skills. Izzy was terrible, but she didn't mind and just rolled her eyes at Lucy and giggled hopelessly every time she had to run off across the field after the ball. Lucy was quite good at sporty stuff, and Mr. Jackson said he'd have to keep an eye on her for the school team. Lucy couldn't help feeling a little excited.

When Lucy's mom came to pick her up she was amazed that Lucy came running across the playground to her, rather than trailing slowly out after everyone else. She was with a pretty, red-haired girl who had a massive grin on her face. The red-haired girl grabbed a tall, red-haired woman, who had to be her own mom, then came to join Lucy.

"Did you ask her?" Izzy said anxiously.

Lucy shook her head. "Mom, please can I go to supper with Izzy? She lives across the street from us. Pleeeaase?"

"Oh, Lucy, that sounds great, but maybe another day?" said Mom. "We haven't given Izzy's mom much notice." She smiled apologetically at the red-haired woman.

"Actually, if you don't mind, it's fine by me," Izzy's mom replied. "Izzy mentioned last night that she'd met Lucy, and she'd love to have her over. Lucky it's a Wednesday. Izzy's sister Amber goes to choir so I pick Izzy up.

Usually the girls walk home together. You've just moved in, haven't you?"

Izzy's mom was really friendly, and as the four of them walked home she told Lucy's mom about the neighbors, and which were the nicest stores in the area.

Izzy's mom made a massive supper of pasta, and afterward Lucy and Izzy hung out in her room. Izzy had a sleepover bed that slid out from underneath hers, and she promised to ask if Lucy could stay the night soon.

"Amber has a portable DVD player. I bet she'd lend it to us for the night," Izzy told her.

Izzy also had a secret stash of chocolate left over from her birthday, and somehow, munching happily and chatting about the worst teachers at their school, Lucy forgot that she wanted to leave Fairford. It seemed all too soon that Izzy's mom was calling up the stairs to say that Lucy's dad was here to take her home.

"See you tomorrow!" Izzy waved

cheerfully to her as she crossed the street. "Hey, ask your mom if you can walk to school with me and Amber!"

Lucy nodded and waved back. "I will, promise!"

Lucy walked into the kitchen, smiling happily to herself, and then stopped. Mom and Dad both had serious faces. "What is it?" she asked anxiously.

"Lucy, Mom and I have been talking. About Sky." Dad's voice was sad as he looked over at Sky's basket.

Lucy looked, too. Sky was curled-up fast asleep—she was so cute.

"We really hoped that having Sky to play with and look after would make you feel better about the move. We know you're missing Ellie and the others." Her dad sighed. "But I'm sure you'll settle down after a while. Izzy seems very nice—it's great that you're starting to make friends."

Where is Dad going with this? Lucy gazed at her parents.

"Anyway, it looks like we made a mistake with Sky. We should have talked to you about it first, before we went ahead and brought her home."

Lucy blinked stupidly. She could see that Dad was telling her something important, but she couldn't quite seem to understand. Sky was a mistake? Lucy started to feel scared. She looked at Sky, who was still asleep in her basket, although she'd wriggled around and was now lying on her back with her paws in the air. She looked like a toy kitten.

Dad smiled sadly as Sky let out a sleepy half-mew, half-purr. "Luckily the breeder we bought Sky from has been very understanding. Tomorrow evening Mom will take Sky back."

Chapter Seven

Lucy felt suddenly cold. It was just like Izzy had said. *You might end up having to stay here, and not having a beautiful kitten.*

"Oh, Lucy, don't look like that!" Her mom came over and gave her a hug. "We're not angry with you. It was our fault for not talking it over with you first."

No, you don't understand! Lucy wanted to cry out. *Don't give her back! I want to keep her!* But her voice seemed to stick in her throat as her parents went on talking.

Mom stroked Lucy's hair sadly. "Sky deserves a home where she's really wanted. She's such a loving little kitten —she needs someone to give her loads of love back."

Lucy had been about to try to explain, but that made her stop. It was so true. Sky did need a home where she was properly loved. Lucy had a horrible feeling that that special home wasn't here with her. She'd been so mean— Sky didn't know whether Lucy loved her or hated her. *Maybe I just don't deserve to have a kitten,* she thought.

But she had to say good-bye to Sky properly. Even if Sky didn't understand.

Later, Lucy crept downstairs while her parents were in the living room. Sky was in the kitchen, as she usually was at night, and Lucy opened the door quietly.

Sky saw her from her basket, and laid her ears slightly back, and stared up as Lucy came closer in the faint light from the hallway.

Lucy gulped. It was obvious that Sky didn't know what was going on. She crouched down by the basket. "Mom and Dad are right," she whispered to the kitten, running one finger down Sky's back. "You do deserve a better home than this. I've come to say good-bye," she murmured, her eyes filling with tears. One of them dripped onto Sky's nose, making her jump.

"Mrow!" she mewed indignantly, and Lucy laughed and cried at the same time, stifling the strange noise in case her parents heard. Sky's face was so funny, her blue eyes round and annoyed.

"Ssshh, Sky!" Lucy scooped Sky up, tucking her into her bath robe. "Come on," she whispered. Lucy looked around quickly as she opened the kitchen door, then scurried up the stairs to her room.

Sky snuggled against Lucy's pajamas, watching curiously as they went upstairs. She'd never gotten this far before, the stairs were steep and someone always caught her before she'd struggled up more than a few steps.

Where was she going? Sky purred excitedly as Lucy opened the door to her room and placed her down gently on the floor.

Lucy snuggled under her comforter and watched Sky exploring her bedroom, sniffing her way around the boxes. Having Sky in her room made the little kitten seem much more *hers*, somehow. Lucy could imagine doing her homework up here, with Sky sitting on her windowsill watching the birds, or snoozing on her comforter. Sky clambered onto the bed next to Lucy, and purred lovingly in her ear.

"What am I going to do, Sky?" Lucy murmured sleepily, stroking her. All of a sudden she was so tired. "I wish you could tell me what to do."

Lucy awoke to find Sky licking her face with her rough little tongue.

"Hey, Sky! That's a nice way to be woken up," she muttered sleepily. "I suppose you want breakfast?" she said, as Sky jumped down off the bed and padded over to the bedroom door.

Lucy threw on her bath robe, and carried Sky downstairs. When they went into the kitchen she jumped lightly down, and stared demandingly at her food bowl. "Mw-wowl!" she told Lucy firmly.

Lucy grabbed the bag of kitten food from the cupboard. She poured some into Sky's bowl, and fetched herself some juice from the fridge.

Watching Sky busily devouring her breakfast, Lucy wondered if she could bear to let Sky go. She was so cute! If she told her parents she'd changed her mind, maybe they could keep her.

Her mom came down a few minutes later. "You fed Sky!" she said in surprise. Then she looked at the bag that Lucy had left on the counter. "I suppose I might as well take that to the breeder's with me later. They'll be able to use it up, or give it to her new owner. The basket and things, too, probably," Mom sighed.

Lucy walked quickly out of the kitchen, before she started to cry. Sky's new owner! The person who was going to really love her. Everything was so complicated, Lucy felt she didn't even know what she wanted any more.

The doorbell rang. Izzy and Amber had come to pick her up for school like they'd arranged last night. Sky peeped around the front door, and Izzy nudged Amber. "Look, isn't she sweet? Isn't Lucy lucky?"

Amber smiled. "Oh! She's so tiny. You really *are* lucky, Lucy!"

Lucy didn't want to explain what had happened in case she started crying again. "Mmmm!" she said, forcing a smile.

As soon as Amber left them at the school gates to go on to her high school, Lucy burst out, "They're taking Sky back!"

"What?" Izzy yelped. "When?"

"Today," Lucy said miserably. "Mom and Dad told me when I got home from your house last night. They said they'd made a mistake, but the people who bred Sky will have her back. Luckily." She sniffed.

Izzy gazed at her in horror. "And you're just going to let them?"

Lucy stared down, noticing that her school skirt had white hairs on it. "I suppose so," she murmured. She was crying *again*!

"You just can't!" Izzy said. "That beautiful kitten, the best present *ever*, and you're letting them take her away!" Izzy's eyes were flashing, and people were staring at them as they walked along the corridor to their classroom.

"You don't understand!" Lucy wailed.

"No, I don't." Izzy dumped her bag on their table.

"Last night I was going to tell them I'd changed my mind about Sky and wanted to keep her," Lucy explained. "I was trying to think how to do it while I was at yours. But when I got home they told me they were going to give Sky back because she needed someone who'd really love her. And they're right! All I've done is make her sad!" she sobbed.

Izzy made a disbelieving noise and put her arm around Lucy. "She didn't look sad the other day when you were cuddling her in your yard! She looked really happy!"

Lucy looked up at her hopefully. "Do you think so?"

Izzy thought for a moment. "Do you think maybe you've been upset about moving house for so long that you're just looking on the wrong side of everything?" she asked.

Lucy felt hurt. It sounded as though Izzy thought she was just being stupid.

"I'm not trying to be mean," Izzy

added hurriedly. "It's just I thought you were actually starting to like being here. You don't *really* hate it, do you?"

Lucy shook her head slowly. "Noooo," she murmured. She looked up at Izzy, feeling confused. She'd been telling herself she hated Fairford for so long, it was hard to admit to someone else that it actually wasn't so bad. "No. Since I made friends with you, it's been fun," she said, smiling. She sat down slowly on the edge of the table, thinking aloud. "And if I could keep Sky, and not have to pretend I didn't like her, it would be even better." Lucy looked shyly up at her friend—Izzy really *was* her friend. "All I have to do is explain to Mom and Dad, and everything will be OK."

Back at Lucy's house, her mom was in the hall searching for her keys, ready to go out shopping. She just had time before Lucy and Kieran came back from school. Mom grabbed her coat from the understairs cupboard. "Where have I put them, puss?" she muttered to Sky. "Oh, there they are, in my pocket all the time!" She sighed, looking at Sky's bright, interested eyes. "I'm going to miss you. But I suppose it's for the best. I'll see you in a while, little one."

Feeling lonely, Sky watched her walk down the street from her perch on the back of the sofa. Then she wandered through the house, looking for something fun to do. She could hear the washing machine rumbling in the kitchen. It would be going around and around! She liked to watch it, so she nudged the door open.

Sky didn't use her basket much during the day—she usually slept on the sofa—so Lucy's mom had tidied it away with her food bowl, and the bag of food. It was all piled up on the counter, ready to take back that evening. Forgetting about the washing machine, Sky looked at the place where her basket was supposed to be, feeling confused. What was going on? Her bowl, her basket, all that food? Didn't they want her anymore?

But she liked it here, and she was sure Lucy was beginning to like having her here, too. Determinedly, Sky stalked out of the kitchen. This was her home now, here with Lucy!

Distracted by losing her keys, Lucy's mom hadn't closed the understairs cupboard properly. Sky had never seen this door open before, not even a crack, and she nudged it farther open with her nose.

It was full of wellington boots and bike helmets and coats, and it looked dark and curious. Sky wriggled through the door, and wove herself between the wellington boots to get farther in. At the back was a big wicker basket, full of scarves and hats. Sky climbed into it, and burrowed under Lucy's fluffy pink hat. Perfect. Now she would stay here until they changed their minds.

Chapter Eight

Lucy and Izzy had agreed to race home after school as fast as they could get Amber to go. As they dashed down their street, Lucy spotted her mom in the driveway, carrying something bulky. It looked awfully like the special box that Sky had come in.

A horrible thought suddenly struck her. What if Mom had taken Sky back earlier than planned? What if Sky had already gone?

She sped ahead of Amber and Izzy, and flung herself through the gates. Her mom had put the box down on the driveway while she closed the garage door, and it was open at the top, its flaps not folded together. It was empty.

Lucy knelt down beside it and looked in, knowing it was no use, but hoping that somehow Sky was there after all, she just wasn't looking properly. But there was no kitten. Lucy was too late. Holding the flaps of the box, Lucy started to cry.

"Lucy!" Her mom was staring at her in horror. "Lucy, what is it? Whatever's the matter?"

Lucy was crying too hard to speak. Izzy and Amber had now caught up with her. Izzy stared down at the box. "Oh no! She's gone already?"

Lucy nodded, her shoulders heaving.

"Girls, what is going on?" Lucy's mom asked.

Izzy looked up at her. "Lucy was going to tell you she didn't want to give Sky back after all. It was all a big mistake."

Lucy's mom gasped. "Lucy? Is this true?" She bent down and pulled Lucy up, putting an arm around her. Lucy clung on to her, still crying quietly.

"Yes," she gulped. "Sorry!"

"But why didn't you say?" her mom asked, confused.

Lucy heaved a shuddering sigh.

"Because I thought you only gave me Sky to make me forget about everyone back home, and I didn't want to forget my friends!"

"That's not why we gave you Sky!" Her mom sounded hurt. "Although I suppose I can understand how you'd see it like that. Oh, Lucy."

"And now it's too late anyway," Lucy sniffed.

Her mom smiled. "Actually it's not."

Lucy looked up at her in sudden hope. "Can we get Sky back?"

"We don't have to. I was just getting the box out of the garage ready, that's all. Sky's inside somewhere. I'm not sure where, I've only been back ten minutes." Lucy's mom smiled as Lucy, Izzy and Amber dashed over to the front door. "Would you like me to let you in, by any chance?"

The girls burst into the house as soon as she opened the door, calling eagerly for Sky, expecting her to come running. Lucy couldn't help thinking how great it was not to have to pretend she didn't care about her wonderful kitten. Her kitten! Sky really was hers now!

"Have you found her?" Lucy's mom called a couple of minutes later, once she'd put the box away. "I'd better phone the breeder and tell her we're not bringing Sky back after all."

But Lucy, Izzy and Amber were coming down the stairs, looking worried.

"What's the matter?" Lucy's mom asked, putting her coat away.

"She's not here," Lucy said anxiously. "She couldn't have gotten out, could she, Mom? She's disappeared. We've looked everywhere."

Her mom closed the cupboard door. "I don't see how she could've gotten out. She was definitely in when I left, I saw her sitting on the back of the sofa as I went out. Come on, let's look again. She's probably hiding, and playing a game with us."

But they looked and looked, and when Kieran got home he joined in, too, and Lucy's dad a while later. By the time Amber had to drag Izzy home for supper, they still hadn't found her. Sky had disappeared completely.

Tucked away in her warm little nest, Sky had heard everyone searching and calling. She'd almost come out, but maybe they were only trying to find her so they could take her away? The voices calling her name sounded frightened and upset. She thought Lucy was crying, and that made her feel sad, too. Maybe she should come out, and make Lucy feel better? It was so hard to know.

Sky wanted her basket to go back in its proper place in the kitchen. If she waited till they all went to bed, maybe she could go and see if they'd put it back for her? Yes, she would come out then. She was awfully hungry, though, and it was a long time to wait.

Sky tunnelled underneath a tasselled

scarf to make her bed more comfortable. The cupboard was chilly, and so lonely. Oh, she wished Lucy would come and find her—the nice Lucy who petted her so lovingly, and told her how beautiful she was. That Lucy didn't want to give her away, she was sure!

"Lucy, I know you want to keep looking, but it's really late. You have to go to bed—you've got school in the morning. We'll search outside tomorrow, even though I still don't see how Sky could have gotten out." Lucy's mom looked anxiously out of the window into the darkness.

Lucy stared out of the window as well, and shivered. It was so dark and cold now. Sky had only been outside the house that once when she'd slipped through the front door. She couldn't stop imagining poor little Sky out there on her own, perhaps hiding under a bush, cold and frightened.

She hugged her mom sadly, then slowly climbed the stairs to her room. Was it only this morning that Sky had woken her up by licking her face? It seemed so long ago. She climbed into bed, and lay there wishing she hadn't been so stupid. If only she'd told her parents sooner that she'd changed her mind, then maybe this wouldn't have happened.

Sky was determined to wait until everyone had gone to bed before she came out. Then she would go and see if they had put her things back in their proper places. If they hadn't, well, she would go back into the cupboard until they did! But she would find something to eat first.

As the noise in the house died down, she cautiously crawled out of her woolly nest and perched at the edge of the basket, her paws on the rim, listening carefully. Could she sneak out and look around yet? Was it safe? Perhaps she could creep up the stairs and see Lucy, too. She missed her so much!

Sky threaded her way carefully across the cupboard, avoiding a pile of umbrellas, and squeaking with disgust as she bumped into Kieran's muddy soccer boots. Here was the door—she could see a line of light shining from the hallway.

But shouldn't that line be bigger?

Sky was horrified as she realized that the door to the cupboard was closed. Confused, she scrabbled desperately at the wood, hoping to make the door open again. This door had definitely been open before. Why was it closed now? She yowled in frustration and fury, her tiny claws leaving long scratches in the paint.

Eventually, Sky's howls turned to frightened cries. She was trapped. She couldn't get out. What if she *never* got out?

Lucy! Come and find me! Please! she mewed.

But everyone else in the house was asleep, tired from searching and crying and worrying, and no one heard.

Eventually, Sky clambered back into her safe little nest. She wriggled under Lucy's hat and fell asleep, her paws sore from scratching.

A little later Lucy woke up with a start. She'd been half-dreaming, half-worrying. What if Sky hadn't just slipped out because she spotted an open door? What if she'd run away on purpose?

Lucy knew she had been behaving oddly, playing with Sky one minute, and ignoring her the next. Maybe Sky had given up on her. After all, she had been taken away from her home and her mom, too, and everything had been different and strange, just like it had been for Lucy.

I drove her away, Lucy thought miserably, certain now that this was what had happened. Suddenly, she threw back her comforter. "I made her go, and it's up to me to go and find her," she muttered to herself. "I can't leave her out there, thinking I don't love her. This is all my fault."

It was past midnight, and Lucy was pretty sure everyone was asleep. She grabbed her flashlight, which luckily was on top of one of her boxes, and sneaked down the stairs. She wasn't going to bother getting dressed—her pajamas were fleecy and warm. She'd just put on her big bath robe, and her fluffy hat and scarf. She was pretty sure Mom had unpacked them, and they were in that cupboard under the stairs.

Inside the cupboard, Sky was in a restless half-sleep. Then all at once the door opened, and a beam of light cut into the gloom of the cupboard, dazzling Sky for a moment before her eyes adjusted. It was Lucy! Sky was about to run to her, when she remembered the way her basket and food bowl were piled up on the kitchen counter. Did Lucy still want her? She peered out from under Lucy's hat, her eyes big and round and hopeful in the dark.

"It's my fault," Lucy whispered to herself. "Poor Sky. All because I was so stubborn."

Sky heard her name, and Lucy's sad voice. But what did it mean?

Lucy spotted the basket, and shone the flashlight over the top, looking for her hat and scarf. It was cold outside and she might be out searching for a while—she wasn't coming back until she'd found Sky and brought her home!

Then she stopped with a gasp. Peering out from under her hat was a tiny creamy-white head. Big blue eyes blinked at her uncertainly.

"Sky!" Lucy breathed. "There you are! Mom was right, you didn't get out after all! Oh, Sky, we've been looking for you all night." She crouched down next to the basket, and looked closely at her. "Are you all right? Were you stuck in here? Why didn't you call?"

Sky watched Lucy warily. Her voice sounded loving, but a little sad as well. *Please don't give me back...* she mewed. *I want to stay!*

"Were you hiding?" Lucy asked slowly. "Because you didn't know what was going on? Oh, Sky, I'm so sorry..." She reached out one finger, very gently, and rubbed Sky under her chin. "It's all going to be fine now, I promise. No more pretending I don't love you, because I really, really do. I know I do. Please come out!"

Sky stood up unsteadily on the pile of hats and gloves, and mewed again. *I'm so hungry!* she told Lucy.

"You must be starved," Lucy muttered. Very gently, she picked Sky up, cradling her close.

Sky could feel Lucy's heart beating as she carried her to the kitchen. Her own heart was thumping anxiously, too. Where would her basket be? She sat tensely in Lucy's arms as she opened the door, and turned on the kitchen light. Then she howled in dismay. It was piled up on the counter still, with her bowl and food bag. They were still going to give her away!

"Hey, hey, Sky, what's wrong?" Lucy asked. "Oh! Your basket. Does it look strange up on the counter like that? It's all right, look." Whispering soothingly and cuddling the tiny kitten in one arm, Lucy took Sky's toys out of the basket and put it back in its warm corner by the radiator. Sky stopped crying, and leaned over Lucy's arm to sniff it suspiciously. It seemed right. Good. Now all Lucy had to do was get her food bowl.

"Lucy!" Lucy's mom was at the kitchen door, her bath robe half-tied, looking worried. "What are you doing?" she said. "Oh, you've found her! Where was she?" She turned to Lucy's dad, who had followed her downstairs. "Lucy's found Sky!"

Lucy carried her kitten over for her mom to pet. "She was in the cupboard under the stairs. She must have been there all that time!" She looked seriously at her parents. "I think she was hiding because she didn't know whether we wanted her or not," she said quietly. "But we really do, don't we?"

"Of course we do," said Mom.

Her dad poured some food into Sky's bowl. "I bet she's starving."

Sky started to eat, gulping down the food, then looking hopefully for more.

"It's not that long till breakfast, Sky, don't worry!" Lucy giggled. She looked up at her mom and dad. "Can Sky sleep on my bed?" she begged.

Her mom nodded. "If you get back to bed right this minute! In fact, I think we should *all* get back to bed!"

Sky rubbed her head against Lucy's chin as she carried her upstairs. She could tell how happy Lucy was.

As Lucy snuggled up under her warm comforter, Sky curled up next to her on the pillow and purred loudly. There was no place either of them would rather be! Lucy and Sky were home.